DON'T WAKE THE YETI!

CLAIRE FREEDMAN

pictures by
CLAUDIA RANUCCI

Albert Whitman & Company
Chicago, Illinois

To my mum with all my love—CF

To Victoria, for being there every time
I need a friend—CR

Library of Congress Cataloging-in-Publication data is on file with the publisher.

Text copyright © 2017 by Claire Freedman
Illustrations copyright © 2017 by Claudia Ranucci
First published in Great Britain in 2017 by Scholastic Children's Books, a division of Scholastic Ltd.
Published in 2017 by Albert Whitman & Company
ISBN 978-0-8075-1690-4

Printed in China
10 9 8 7 6 5 4 3 2 1 LP 22 21 20 19 18 17

For more information about Albert Whitman & Company,
visit our website at www.albertwhitman.com.

If you think there's a yeti under your bed, don't scream or panic. Don't lose your head. As yetis, you know, are incredibly rare...

first check that it's not something else hiding there.

Like those polar bear slippers you kicked on the floor,

or the blanket that Mom couldn't fit in the drawer.

Uh-oh—so you've checked,
and it's not this or that,
and the furry white mound
is too huge for a cat.

Oh, yikes–it's a yeti!
But here's the good news:
those loud snuffly snores mean he's having a snooze.
You've got time to think of the next step to take...

You've given the yeti a terrible fright.
Tell him you're sorry. Say humans don't bite!

But if he still finds your lampshade appealing,
show him it's safe to come down from the ceiling.

After he's eaten, he'll need a COLD bath.
He'll wear your mom's shower cap (please try not to laugh).

Fill the tub with ice cubes,
but don't even try
to stay in the room
when he shakes himself dry.

Of course when you tell him,

"Off to school! Can't be late!"

he'll beg to go with as your brand-new classmate.

The teacher might think he's your show-and-tell pet.
Your friends will gasp, "WOW! He's the funniest one yet!"

He'll eat all the slugs on the playground—Ugh! Yuck!

And don't let him loose on the slide—he'll get stuck!

You should be aware—if you take Yeti shopping,
he'll munch all the food till his tummy is popping.

Then he'll squeeze in the freezer (as yetis love snow)

and make a great fuss when you say, "Time to go!"

All yetis, unfortunately,
have TONS of fleas—

they tickle his tummy
and big knobbly knees.

He'll ask you to scratch him
for itchy relief.

Take note! If he **eats** some,
you **must** brush his teeth.

By now you'll be asking,
"Help! What will Mom say?"

"A huge hairy yeti—
he can't stay here! No way!"

The fact is that yetis are great at disguise.

He's a chair,

then a rug—

in a flash of Mom's eyes.

Though keeping a yeti won't suit everyone,
they're cuddly and silly. They're friendly and fun.
And things could be MUCH worse, if under your bed...

You find a huge **dinosaur** hiding instead!